Balboa Press books may be ordered through booksellers or by contacting:

Balboa Press
A Division of Hay House
1663 Liberty Drive
Bloomington, IN 47403
www.balboapress.com.au
1 (877) 407-4847

Because of the dynamic nature of the Internet, any web addresses or links contained in this book may have changed since publication and may no longer be valid. The views expressed in this work are solely those of the author and do not necessarily reflect the views of the publisher, and the publisher hereby disclaims any responsibility for them.

Any people depicted in stock imagery provided by Getty Images are models, and such images are being used for illustrative purposes only. Certain stock imagery © Getty Images.

ISBN: 978-1-5043-1613-2 (sc)
ISBN: 978-1-5043-1614-9 (e)

Print information available on the last page.

Balboa Press rev. date: 12/29/2018

Mum,
The Fairies
Stole my Glasses

As Sally woke, she reached out and grabbed her glasses from the bedside cabinet.

She pushed them over her nose and around her ears.

Now, Sally could see her bedroom clearly.

She jumped off her bed and ran over to the mirror.

Sally poked her tongue out at the mirror as she pulled out clothes out from her chest of drawers.

She tried every t-shirt, but none of them went with her glasses.

Sally took off her glasses and flung them away as she twirled around the room.

And now, her t-shirts suited her just fine.

Sally rushed downstairs and skipped
all the way to the kitchen.

"Where are your glasses, Sally?" Mum asked.
"You go back upstairs and put them on as
soon as you've finished breakfast."

She nodded her head and sat down for breakfast.
Sally finished her cereal and skipped down the
hallway to play. But she bumped into a door.

"Ouch, that hurt. Stupid door," Sally groaned.

"Go and put your glasses on now, Sally,"
Mum shouted from the kitchen.

Sally frowned and blew a big fat raspberry
before bouncing up the stairs.

Sally jumped around her bedroom as
she looked for her glasses.

"I know they're here somewhere," Sally said,

throwing her teddy across the room.

"I can't find them, Mum," Sally shouted.

Mum stood at the doorway of Sally's room,

looking at all the mess, and sighed.

"Why can't you find them?" Mum asked.

"I put them on the side of my bed

last night, Mum," Sally said.

"If you put them on your bedside cabinet they

would still be there, Sally," Mum said.

"I think the fairies must have taken them," Sally muttered.

"I don't think so, Sally. You will stay in your

bedroom until you find your glasses."

"But mum, the fairies stole my glasses—look—strange footprints on my window sill," Sally whispered.

Mum carefully studied the footprints on the window sill. She frowned and shook her head.

"By the time I come back, Sally, I want this room tidy," Mum said, closing the door behind her.

Sally picked up her t-shirts and shoved them in the drawers.

She picked up her teddies and put them on the chair.

She searched under the chair but only found yucky fluff.

She put her shoes in the cupboard and thought she had better search there.

But sitting on the floor, she came to the only conclusion possible.

"The fairies stole my glasses," she whispered to her teddies.

Mum came back at lunchtime with Dad.

"I still can't find my glasses, Mum. I know the fairies have stolen them."

Sally showed her Dad the window sill.

Shaking his head, Dad studied the strange footprints. Scratching his head, he looked out the window and over the garden.

Dad looked at Mum and Mum looked at Dad. They both shook their heads.

"These are very strange footprints. I wonder what really happened to your glasses, Sally," Dad said.

Sally shrugged her shoulders.

Sally could not go out to play because she could not see properly without her glasses. She could not read her favorite book because she could not properly see the words.

She searched her room again and again. But she was sure the fairies had stolen her glasses.

She had a headache because she did not wear her glasses all week.

She went to bed early and missed her favorite cartoon shows.

Sally was so sad all week.

On Saturday, Dad handed Sally a bright red glass case.

"Make sure you look after these glasses, Sally. The optometrist made them especially for you."

She opened the bright red case and squinted hard. She touched them all over with her fingers.

"Thank you, Dad. I promise I won't let the fairies steal them."

She slipped her new glasses over her nose and round her ears.

She ran up the stairs and into her bedroom.

She looked at herself in the mirror. Her bright red glasses had tiny kangaroos at the corners of each lens.

"I look amazing," Sally announced, running out of her room and down the stairs.

"What if the fairies come and steal these glasses, mum?" Sally asked.

"I don't think the fairies will come and take these new glasses, Sally."

When Sally went to bed that night, she took off her glasses and slipped them back into the bright red case. She looked around her bedroom and pushed the case under her pillow.

"I wonder what happened to my yucky glasses," Sally muttered. "I wonder if the fairies really did take them. It's a real mystery."

A message from the author:

"I know what happened to Sally's glasses. Would you like to know?"

When Sally was dancing, she had thrown them across the room, and they had landed on the back of a possum sitting on the window sill. The possum climbed down the drain and jumped on the tree outside Sally's window. She shook herself hard, and the glasses fell and landed in a crow's nest. They made Mrs. Crow's eggs look out of shape, and she pushed them out of her nest.

And the glasses landed on a bush.

A week later, Tommy the cat was walking through the bush, and the glasses caught his long ginger fur. He climbed up the tree and jumped all the way over to Sally's window.

Tommy preened and cleaned and scratched himself clean. Finally, as he shook his fluffy fur, the glasses flew free and twirled through the air and landed with a bump on Sally's bedside cabinet.

When Sally woke the next morning, she felt

for her new glasses under the pillow.

She pulled out the bright red glasses and slipped

them over her nose and around her ears.

She yawned as she looked at her

bedside cabinet and screamed.

"Mum—the fairies didn't like my yucky

glasses either, they've brought them back."

Printed in the United States
By Bookmasters